In memory of a wonderful pet, little Charlie, who will always be missed.
This book is dedicated to Jack Merstik
who loved and took such excellent care of Charlie.

Book Designer: Emily J. Green

To order additional copies of this book, contact:
Xlibris
844-714-8691
www.Xlibris.com
Orders@Xlibris.com

ISBN: Softcover   978-1-4134-4200-7
        Hardcover   978-1-4134-4199-4

Library of Congress Control Number: 2004099861

Print information available on the last page

Rev. date: 12/15/2021

The Little Throw-Away Dog

Written by Carmen Merstik
Illustrated by Aura Hogue

"What is a throw-away dog?" you ask.

There are dogs who get lost... Their families look for them, miss them a lot and are very happy when they find them.

There are dogs who run away and can't find their way home and they are missed too. The families of these dogs are very sad without their pets.

This story is about a little dog who was not loved or wanted by his owners... a little throw-away dog, until he found a new home.

The man first saw him when he stepped out into the parking lot where he worked. The little dog looked very scared and ran quickly to hide under a car.

He was dirty and probably hungry. There were no houses in this neighborhood so he probably had lived far from there and walked a long way.

There was a lot of traffic too, so he was lucky he had not been hit by a car.

The man went to the dairy next door and bought cat food because they had no dog food. He opened it and put it near the car and walked away.

In a little while, the dog came out slowly, looked all around and started eating. Even though his reddish-blond long hair and his paws and short legs were dirty, he was a really cute dog. He had big dark eyes, a little nose and a little, very pink tongue.

The man was afraid something bad would happen to the little dog during the night if he left him there...

so... he decided to take him home and look for his owners but he was not able to find them.

He and his wife decided to keep the little dog because they liked him a lot and they named him Charlie. It did not take long for them to start loving him very much.

Everyone who saw him said he was "just the cutest dog!"

And, he was!

Charlie was about a year and a half old when he came to this new home. He grew to be a very happy dog. His new family took very good care of him and he gave them lots of love.

Charlie liked to jump and could jump higher than any dog his new family had ever seen, especially one with such short legs... even the man who lived next door was amazed at the way Charlie would jump straight up into his master's arms.

He needed a lot of attention and love. He liked to sit on the man's lap as they watched television or listened to music...

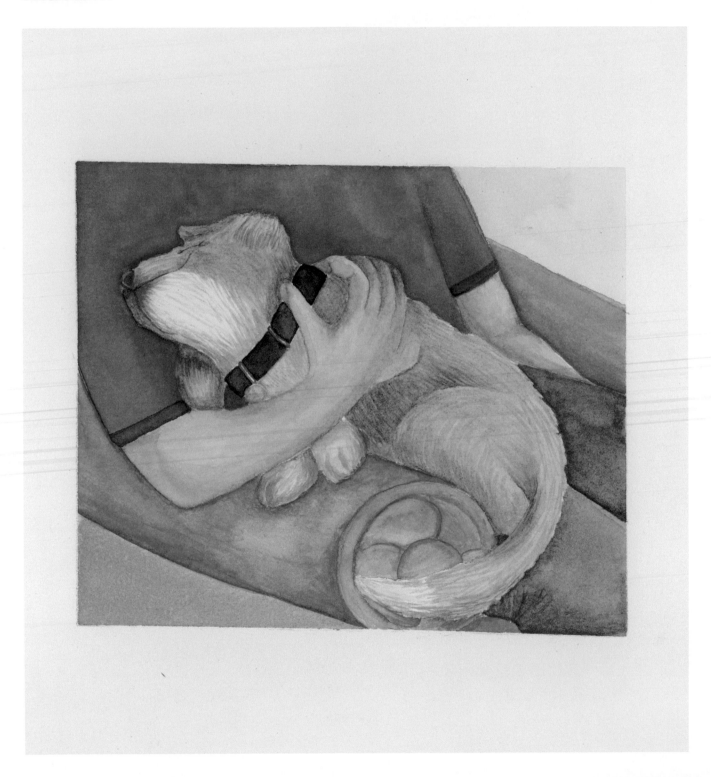

... he was always around his new master.

When the man went to the hospital for surgery, Charlie missed him a lot and when his master came home, the little dog jumped up onto his bed which was very high and kept him company.

He snuggled very close to him and licked the man's hands and looked very happy.

He was part of the family and included in everything. He had lots of new toys and played ball and other games with the man. He ran in the back yard and used his doggie door to go in and out of the house when he was home alone.

He slept a lot, too, and sometimes had dreams...

...and even barked a little in his sleep.

This always made the man and the woman smile and wonder what he was dreaming about.

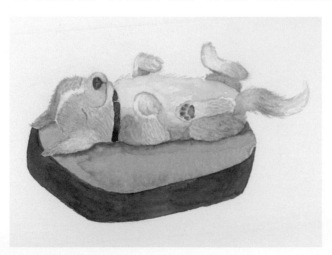

He was just the best little dog and they were happy he was part of their family.

Charlie had lived with his family for more than 15 years when his owners realized that he was having more and more trouble walking.

Then they noticed that he couldn't see and hear too well. They had to carry him a lot now. They were worried about him and took him to see his veterinarian and got him special medicine to help him a little.

They went to see a specialist about his eyes but the doctor told them that the problem was caused by his age and there was no cure for the things that were wrong with him. This made them sad because they understood that Charlie might not be with them much longer.

They gave him a lot of love and took very good care of him... even better care than they had before.

The doctor had told them that he had a strong heart and was a real little fighter.

But the day that they had worried
and been sad about came...

Charlie had been spending more and more time sleeping and had been having more trouble walking, seeing and hearing. And on that day, he spent almost the whole day just sleeping and looking sad.

His family knew that he probably would not get better. During the night, they decided they would take him to see his vet in the morning, to get some advice.

The man stayed up all night with little Charlie, holding him in his arms and on his lap. Sadly, little Charlie was not meant to get better and just after it got light that morning, he looked up at the man one last time and left for a place where little animals feel good all the time... and run... and play... and sleep...

Little Charlie had died.

The man and the woman felt very sad and cried because they loved him and they knew that they would miss him very much for a very long time.

As little as he was, he had a big, big place in their hearts and their lives...

They were happy too for Charlie because now he wasn't sick anymore. They felt both sad and happy when they closed their eyes and imagined Charlie running and playing just like when he was a little puppy!

The man and the woman wished they could have more time with their little Charlie but they were... oh so happy... because of the good times spent with him. They knew they would always remember him with love!

It hurts a lot to lose a special pet but Charlie's family knew that they had loved him and taken good care of him. They knew that he had been a happy little dog.

Will they ever get another dog? It's too soon to think about it but maybe if one as special as Charlie comes along...

... maybe another little throw-away dog?

The End

Printed in the United States
by Baker & Taylor Publisher Services